CREATURES

SPIDER FRIGHT

ED GRAVES

■SCHOLASTIC

First published in the UK in 2010 by Scholastic Children's Books
An imprint of Scholastic Ltd
Euston House, 24 Eversholt Street
London, NW1 1DB, UK
Registered office: Westfield Road, Southam, Warwickshire, CV47 0RA
SCHOLASTIC and associated logos are trademarks and/or registered
trademarks of Scholastic Inc.
Series created by Working Partners Ltd

Text copyright © Working Partners, 2010
The right of Ed Graves to be identified as the author of this work
has been asserted by him.

ISBN 978 1407 11714 0

Printed in the UK by CPI Bookmarque, Croydon, Surrey.
Papers used by Scholastic Children's Books are made
from wood grown in sustainable forests.

1 3 5 7 9 10 8 6 4 2

www.scholastic.co.uk/zone

With special thanks to Tracey Turner

For Tom, Toby and the Water Parrots

This Book Belongs To

The Gnome of Gnome Gardens
_ _ _ _ _ _ _ _ _ _ _ _ _ _ _

Beware!

Never open my Book, unless you

want the Curse of Gnome upon you.

Or is it too late?

Then my creatures will terrify

and torment you.

You can't imagine how scared you will be.

Gnome Gardens belongs to me.

Only me. You shall see. . .

CHAPTER ONE

Shifting Shadows

What's that?

Jamie walked into the ancient nursery in Gnome Gardens. He saw a dark shape scuttle through the shadows. His hand shaking, he flicked on the light switch — but the shape disappeared. The room was perfectly still. The only movement came from the ivy blowing in the wind outside, tapping at the windows like ghostly fingers.

Jamie shook himself.

Two pairs of footsteps echoed up the stairs.

"Hurry up!" called Jamie. "I've found the perfect room for our midnight feast." He wouldn't tell the others about whatever it was he'd spotted in the dark – no point in ruining the evening's adventure.

"We're coming!" Jamie's brother, Harry, shouted back.

"*You* try hauling this stuff up two flights of stairs!" Milly called. Jamie and Harry had met Milly, their next-door neighbour, when they'd moved in.

The old nursery was a huge, dusty room at the top of the house. By the fireplace, a rocking horse with a bedraggled mane and tail stared at the floor with dull painted eyes. An ancient chest of drawers leaned against one wall, and next to it was a dolls' house, nearly as tall as Jamie. The dolls' house reminded Jamie of Gnome Gardens – grey, sprawling and run-down, with turrets and gargoyles, like a picture of a haunted house in a book.

Jamie and Harry had arrived at Gnome Gardens a few weeks ago. The house used to belong to their granddad, who'd spent years alone here writing his books, including his famous *Book of Gnome*. Jamie and Harry had been fed up with hearing about it – until they found the original copy of *The Book of Gnome*. That ancient book held a terrifying secret. An evil Gnome had put a curse on this house!

Harry appeared in the doorway with Milly. They were both wearing pyjamas, just like Jamie. Harry's had cartoon trains all over them. Milly's pyjamas had grey-and-white stripes – she didn't like anything fussy – and her hair was in two long plaits. They peered at Jamie from behind the pile of sheets, sleeping bags, duvets and pillows they were carrying, then dumped everything on the floor and looked around. Milly brushed the hair out of her face, her cheeks glowing.

"That thing's creepy," said Harry, pointing at the dolls' house.

"No, it's not," said Milly, picking up a sheet and shaking it out. "It's only an old toy. We can use it to make a tent."

She draped the sheet between the dolls'

4

house roof and the chest of drawers, tucking a corner into one of the drawers. She used another sheet to make a flap for the entrance, tucking that into a drawer too. Finally, she opened the flap and sat inside her tent, looking pleased with herself.

"That's brilliant," Jamie said, impressed.

"And look, I brought this." Milly unrolled a sleeping bag and took out something that looked like a rocket. She plugged it into a socket by the dolls' house. The rocket lit up, casting a green glow inside the tent, then yellow, then red. Inside it, globules of liquid rose to the top, forming swirling shapes. The shapes cast strange shadows before they slowly sank to the bottom again.

"What's that?" Harry asked. "How does it work?"

"It's called a lava lamp," Milly said proudly. "It's got wax in it, which gets heated up and moves."

Harry went to examine it more closely. "It's making weird shapes on the walls," he said.

Jamie thought one of the shadows looked like a giant, swaying snake. He ducked inside the tent and started arranging sleeping bags, duvets and pillows. "Come on, Harry."

His brother crawled in, carrying a duvet. He was wearing the same backpack he took everywhere.

"What's in your survival kit this time?" Jamie asked, smiling. "I knew you'd bring it along. After all, everyone knows midnight feasts are *really* dangerous."

"You never know. Not in this house," said

Harry. He brought out a bag of crisps, a pair of Dad's gardening gloves, a small plastic bucket and spade, still covered in sand from their last trip to the beach, and a net bag of shiny gold chocolate coins. Then he turned the backpack upside down and shook it. "That's funny," he said, frowning. "I'm sure I put my silver car in here."

"Your favourite one?" Jamie asked.

Harry nodded.

"It'll turn up. Anyway, I'm glad you brought the crisps and chocolate. If Mum's mountain of snacks runs out, they'll be our emergency supplies!"

"What emergency?" asked Harry in a small voice. Jamie rolled his eyes.

"You can tease now," Milly said, "but you weren't laughing the last time we needed

Harry's survival kit. We'd never have got away from the Gnome and his snakes without his toy trumpet."

The three of them fell silent. Jamie shivered as he remembered being attacked by a mass of writhing, hissing snakes, wrapping their coils around his arms and legs. But even the snakes hadn't been as terrifying as their master, the evil Gnome.

"Did you tell your parents about what happened?" asked Milly.

Jamie shook his head. "They'd never believe it. *I* wouldn't believe it if I hadn't been there."

"My mum thought my clothes were filthy from playing by the river," said Milly. "She—"

A yelp from Harry interrupted her.

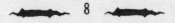

"What's that?" Harry was pointing through the tent flap towards the dolls' house. Something was moving inside one of the bottom windows.

I was right, thought Jamie. *There is something in the nursery. . .*

A long, hairy leg reached through the window, feeling for the floor. Another leg poked out, and another. An enormous, hairy spider, as big as Jamie's hand, struggled out and squatted on a dusty floorboard.

"Urgh!" Harry shrank back.

Jamie remembered the words in the *Book of Gnome* about the next creature they would meet: *Beware the spider's embrace.* Had this spider been sent by the Gnome? Jamie grabbed the plastic spade and tapped it sharply on the floorboard in front of the creature. It scuttled towards the wall and squeezed underneath a gap in the skirting board.

Harry shuddered and moved back further into the tent. He patted his backpack. "See?" he said. "My survival kit saved us again!"

"Shhhh!" Milly put her finger to her lips. "Listen."

The stairs creaked, one by one. Someone was climbing them, slowly.

Creak.

"It's the Gnome!" said Harry desperately.

They looked at one another. There was a pause.

Creak.

The footsteps were moving across the landing, towards the nursery. In the crack of light under the door, Jamie could see the shadowy outline of two feet. His heart pounded as he heard fingers scrabbling at the door handle. He grabbed the plastic spade, holding it before him like a sword as the handle began to turn. . .

CHAPTER TWO

A Fearful Feast

The door screeched on its hinges as it swung slowly open. Jamie held his breath, his fingers clenched tightly round the spade.

"Here, give us a hand," said Mum, pushing the door open with her shoulder. Jamie let out a long breath of relief. He got up and crossed the room to take the tray she was carrying. It groaned under the weight of iced buns, crisps, jelly, cheese sandwiches, plates, cups and a flask of what Jamie hoped was hot chocolate. He bent down and passed the tray inside the tent. Mum ducked her head in and handed round the plates. "Have you two been in the kitchen?" she asked Jamie and Harry as she laid down the sandwiches. "I can't find my cheese grater anywhere."

"No, Mum," said Jamie and Harry together. *Another thing that's gone missing*, Jamie thought.

"Never mind," said Mum. "Are you all right, Milly?"

Milly nodded.

"Don't let these two keep you awake with their scary stories. I know what they're like," she said.

Mum crawled back out of the tent and crossed the room to the light switch. But just as she reached out her hand, the bulb in the overhead light flickered and died. The room dimmed, lit only by the glow of the lava lamp and a sliver of moon shining through the window. The lamp's eerie green glow made Mum look ghoulish. Jamie shuddered. The lava lamp's light changed from green, to yellow, to red: the Gnome's colours.

"I must replace that bulb tomorrow. Sweet dreams!" Mum said, pausing at the door. "Not scared, are you? Goodnight!"

"Goodnight!" they chorused back as she closed the nursery door behind her. But the words stuck in Jamie's throat. His mum had no idea of the scares they'd already had in this house.

Harry hugged his backpack. "Do you think the Gnome will appear tonight?" he asked. "What if he does? We'd better be ready for him."

"Lucky I brought this, then," Jamie said, lifting a pillow to reveal an old, dusty book with a laughing gnome on the front cover. It was the *Book of Gnome*. "I sneaked it up from the study this afternoon."

"The first page in the book showed the snake," said Milly. "Let's have another look at the spider picture. It might help."

Jamie opened the book's heavy covers and turned the pages. Harry and Milly peered over his shoulders.

The lamp cast its eerie light over a picture of the monstrous, hairy spider. Eight red eyes stared out at them and the spider's dagger-like teeth glinted silver. Jamie shuddered. He read the words aloud: "*Beware the spider's embrace.*"

Harry gulped. "I hate spiders," he said. "The Gnome's spider will be huge. Look at those teeth. Do you think it'll trap us in a giant web? We'd be like helpless insects, just stuck there, waiting—"

"Harry, don't," said Milly. She took the book from Jamie and snapped it firmly shut, sending a cloud of dust puffing into the air between them. "We need to be ready for the Gnome, but frightening ourselves isn't going to do any good."

"Milly's right," said Jamie.

"Anyway," she continued, "there's no point in wasting our feast. Come on." She reached towards a plate. Jamie noticed that her hand was trembling, despite everything she'd said.

"It's not midnight yet, though," Harry began.

Milly held the plate of iced buns under his nose. Harry smiled, picked one up and took a huge bite. Milly helped herself to a sandwich.

Jamie didn't feel hungry. His stomach churned as he imagined meeting the horrible spider in the book. But he took a bun anyway and bit into it, forcing himself to smile. The sickly-sweet icing stuck to the roof of his mouth.

"Here," said Milly, pouring hot chocolate from the flask into cups.

Jamie didn't feel like drinking sweet hot chocolate either, but he took a cup.

Tap. Tap. Scratch.

They all stopped chewing. Jamie gulped down his mouthful of iced bun. Harry and Milly were staring around the room, their startled faces bathed in the coloured lamplight.

"Is it the Gno—" Harry began, but Jamie put a finger to his lips.

Scratch. Tap. Tap.

There it was again. It sounded like tiny claws scrabbling right underneath them, below the floorboards.

A blob of quivering jelly plopped from Milly's spoon onto her plate. Her face was deathly pale.

"What *is* that?" whispered Jamie.

CHAPTER THREE

A Night Creature

The scratching noise stopped; everything became still and quiet. *I have to be brave,* Jamie told himself. He peered out between the sheets. The dolls' house and chest of drawers looked exactly the same. The rocking horse stared at the floor by the fireplace. *Just an empty, dusty room.*

Bang!

A window swung open, knocking loudly against the wall, making the glass panes rattle in the frame.

"Jamie." Milly's white face appeared beside him. "It's the Gnome, isn't it?"

"I don't know," Jamie whispered back. "But I'm going to close the window in case he tries to come in." He felt goosebumps prickle on his arms as he crawled outside the tent. He crept over to the window.

A cold gust of wind rushed in. The curtains flapped in the icy blast, and Jamie leapt to press himself against the wall. The rocking horse began to move, creaking back and forth. Jamie watched, frozen with fear. It might be just the wind making the horse move. Or was it the work of the Gnome?

Gritting his teeth, Jamie tried to move towards the window again, but another great gust of wind came howling into the room. It hit Jamie in the chest like a punch, throwing him to the floor. The wind swept round the room, pulling at the tent and blowing one of the sheets to the floor, overturning cups and plates, and slamming the lamp to the ground. The rocking horse lurched wildly, its runners creaking. Harry and Milly sheltered underneath what was left of the tent.

"Jamie!" shouted Milly from beneath the sheets. "You've got to close the window before it gets worse."

"I'm trying!" Jamie yelled back. He crawled across the floor, battling against the wind that still howled into the room. He reached up. . .

Whoosh! Something black flew in out of the night. Small, sharp claws whipped over Jamie's head, grazing his hair. He fell to the floor, throwing his arms over his head. His heart pounded against his chest. Then the wind dropped and the room became still again.

"What was that *thing*?" Harry said, his voice squeaking.

Trembling, Jamie turned and peered around the room. He made out a black shape fluttering near the ceiling.

Harry and Milly crawled out from under the collapsed tent, and they all stared at one another in the lamplight. Something was crashing around the room, scratching the walls, clattering against the windows, door and walls.

"It's one of the Gnome's creepy creatures," wailed Harry. "I just know it!"

The dark shape began swooping around the room. It collided with a wall, knocked over the remains of the tent, and flung the roof from the dolls' house. Harry pulled a duvet over his head. Milly hugged her arms around herself, her shoulders hunched.

Just as suddenly as it had burst into the room, the thing stopped moving. Jamie could hear his heart pounding as he listened, trying to work out where it was.

"Has it gone?" said Harry, emerging from the duvet.

"*Caaaw!*"

Jamie looked at the others, relief washing over him.

Milly was smiling. "It's just a bird! I thought so all along. Come on."

They scrambled over the pile of sheets and duvets. There, on the head of the rocking horse, perched a jackdaw, its head cocked, bright eyes glinting in the coloured light. It was hopping nervously from one foot to the other.

"Poor thing," said Milly, "it's frightened." She slowly crossed the room towards the bird. Jamie turned the lava lamp the right way up.

The jackdaw eyed Milly suspiciously.

"It's all right, bird," she said. "You'll be free in a minute." Slowly, making soft clucking noises, she stretched out her hand towards it. . .

Whooosh! A swirl of icy wind snatched

up the bird. It gave a terrified squawk and, with a horrible sucking sound, it vanished up the chimney.

Jamie, Harry and Milly stared at the fireplace. A single black feather drifted down into the grate.

"How did that happen? What could have sucked the bird up the chimney?" said Harry.

"It must be the Gnome," Jamie said in a whisper.

The three of them went over to the fireplace and warily peered up into the darkness. Jamie brushed aside a thick, sticky cobweb from the mantelpiece: just like the other wooden surfaces in Gnome Gardens, it was decorated with carvings of plants and animals. Beetles scuttled over thorny branches, waving sharp pincers. A carved scorpion raised its tail, the deadly sting poised. Centipedes and fat slugs crawled and slithered down either side of the hearth. *At least there aren't any spider carvings*, Jamie thought, remembering the stone snakes coming to life the last time they'd met the Gnome.

"*Caaaw!*" The jackdaw's cry echoed mournfully down the chimney.

"We can't leave it up there," said Jamie, frowning.

"I've an idea," said Milly. "In our cottage there's a fireplace just like this. It has a ladder inside it, so someone can climb up to sweep it. I bet there's one here, too."

Jamie trembled as he reached up inside the dark chimney. It felt cool and damp.

Sure enough, his hand closed around the cool metal of a bottom rung.

"Come on," he said, ducking into the fireplace and taking hold of the ladder. "Let's rescue the bird."

CHAPTER FOUR

Twisted Tunnels

"Hang on," Harry said, hanging back. "The Gnome must have done that to the bird. He *wants* us to go up there. He could suck us up too! He'll trap us."

Milly peered up the chimney again. "Look, Harry," she said. "You can see the moon at the top. If the Gnome were up there, we'd be able to see him."

Harry looked. "I'm not sure," he said.

"Come on, we can't leave the bird up there," said Jamie.

"What about the Gnome's spider?" Harry shuddered. "It's the perfect place for it to get us!"

"But there's a frightened animal up there," Milly said. "Anyway, we'll soon get it out."

"*Caaw!*" The jackdaw sounded panicky.

They all jumped as the window swung wide open, crashing into the wall. Another gust of cold wind whipped round the room, sending the rocking horse swaying and tugging at their pyjamas like icy fingers.

"Not again!" cried Harry. "I don't like it."

"We'll be sheltered inside the chimney," said Jamie, passing Harry his backpack.

Jamie swung himself onto the ladder, his hands and bare feet cold on the metal rungs. The air inside the chimney smelt musty and stale, but at least it wasn't windy. Milly and Harry were close behind. The chimney flue became narrower as they climbed and it was filthy. In the dim moonlight, Jamie could see smudges of soot and sticky cobwebs all over his pyjamas.

"You two all right?" he called down to the others.

"Ow!" shouted Harry. "Milly stood on my hand."

"Sorry," said Milly.

Jamie felt the sticky touch of a thick

cobweb against his face and brushed it away, shuddering.

The jackdaw squawked from somewhere above them and Jamie could hear it flapping its wings in panic. He felt a sprinkling of soot on his head. "Don't worry, bird!" he called. "We're coming!"

"If we can chase it up the flue, it'll fly out through the top of the chimney," Milly called.

Jamie looked up, to where the moon should have been shining through the chimney, but all he could see was the dark.

"Where's the moon gone?" called Harry from below.

"There's just a cloud over it," said Milly.

She's probably right, thought Jamie. But without the moonlight it was even darker than before. He felt for the next rung: there was nothing there. He found himself clutching at thin air, his legs swinging as he lost his grip on the ladder.

"Hold on!" called Milly. He felt her grab his ankle. She guided his foot back onto a rung.

"Thanks," panted Jamie. He felt the wall above the top rung of the ladder until his fingers closed over a round stone sticking out from the brickwork. He held onto the stone for support, and felt around higher up. There were more round stones.

"There's no more ladder," he called down the chimney. "There are ledges to climb up instead."

"Careful, Jamie!" called Harry.

Jamie didn't reply. He was peering through

the near darkness at one of the stones. With a horrible shiver, Jamie realized that it wasn't just a lump of rock. It had been sculpted into a fat, round body. He counted eight legs and, at the top, a pair of pincers. As Jamie's eyes adjusted to the gloom, he could see that all the footholds were stone spiders.

"What's wrong?" asked Milly.

"Nothing," said Jamie quickly. But he felt suddenly cold. And what had happened to the bird? It had stopped squawking. He gulped and reached up for the next spider-shaped stone, but this time there were two of them, leading in different directions. He raised his hand, feeling through the darkness above his head. The chimney opening was closed over; in its place were two tunnels, jutting sideways. One was heading right, and one left.

It's impossible, he thought to himself. *When we started climbing, we could see the moon in the sky. How could the inside of the chimney have changed?*

"Jamie?" Milly called. "Why have you stopped?"

"We can't climb up any further," he explained. "There are two tunnels."

"What?" Milly asked, sounding puzzled.

"I knew there was something wrong with this place," Harry said. "It must be the Gnome."

Jamie felt something brush against his face: not a cobweb this time, but a feather, drifting down from the right-hand passage, and the faint sound of a desperate caw. "That was the bird again," he said. "Come on – at least we know which tunnel to take."

He pulled himself up into the tunnel on the right, and turned to help Milly and Harry climb after him.

It was easier to crawl along the tunnel than climb up the chimney, but it was even darker than before. Jamie moved carefully, struggling to see. The bricks were gritty and rough under his hands and knees, and cobwebs trailed against his skin and hair with a horrible sticky touch. He ducked to squeeze under a wooden beam.

"I think we're in the roof of the house," he said over his shoulder.

There were scratching and scuttling sounds all around them.

"What's making that noise?" Harry asked.

"Just little insects and mice," said Milly.

Jamie could hear a slight tremble in her voice.

Squelch! A horrible sucking noise echoed through the tunnel.

"W-what's that, then?" stammered Harry as the sound faded away.

Something clung to Jamie's face: a cobweb as thick as rope, with several feathers stuck to it. "Urgh!" he cried out, flicking the web away with his hand. It stuck to the side of the tunnel, where it oozed silvery slime.

"A cobweb like that wasn't made by a normal spider," said Milly grimly. "The Gnome's creature must be nearby."

More feathers wafted along the tunnel, filling the dusty air.

"Are they the bird's?" Harry asked. Jamie could hear the misery in his voice. A caw rang out, but seemed to turn into a snarling laugh. . .

"The Gnome!" Milly cried. "We've been tricked."

"I want to go back," Harry begged, his voice trembling. "We should never have come up here."

Harry's frightened voice sent guilt plunging through Jamie. Why had it ever seemed like a good idea to help the bird? "Come on," he said, "let's go."

As they turned to scramble back along the narrow tunnel, Milly gave a cry.

"Look!" she said. "Something's shining over there."

Jamie could see a gleam of silver in the darkness, behind a stack of roof tiles. Milly reached forward to pick the object up. It was a small pair of bright silver scissors, the handle decorated with a glittering red jewel.

"What are these doing up here in the roof?" said Milly, turning the scissors over in her hand.

Jamie remembered Harry's missing silver car and Mum's cheese grater. Was the Gnome stealing their things? Maybe he'd stolen the scissors, too.

Suddenly the church bells clanged out into the night. Jamie counted the chimes. Midnight.

"That's when the stone snakes came to life," said Milly, the whites of her eyes glowing in the darkness.

"Let's get out of here," Jamie said, "before we end up like that poor bird!"

CHAPTER FIVE

Caught in the Cobwebs

Jamie could feel cold sweat trickling down his forehead as they scrambled back along the tunnel. Ahead, he could make out the round shape of a spider foothold. "Almost at the chimney," he panted.

A loud rasping noise echoed around them,

like the sound of bricks scraping together. They stopped. The tunnel seemed to be shaking.

"What's happening?" said Harry, his voice thick with fear.

The sound grew louder. To Jamie's horror, the tunnel began to move. It shifted violently, twisting one way, then another.

"Jamie!" Harry cried, as the movement flung them against the tunnel wall.

Trickles of dust poured from the ceiling and the floor lurched underneath them. They huddled together, their cries ringing out over the terrible grinding and rumbling. *The house is going to collapse*, Jamie thought.

At last the noise began to drop. The tunnel stopped twisting and turning and seemed to rock like a boat at sea, then gradually stopped.

"Is everyone all right?" Jamie asked. They were all coughing in the dusty air. Through the darkness, Jamie could just make out Milly and Harry nodding their heads, both of them covered in dust and grime.

"We must be almost at the chimney," said Jamie. He crawled forward along the tunnel, feeling in front of him. But he couldn't find the stone spiders.

"Don't you see?" said Milly. "The tunnel's changed, just like the chimney did – we can't go back the way we came."

"Then how are we going to get out of here?" Harry asked, panic in his voice.

Jamie's heart pounded.

"What are we going to do?" Harry was

tugging at Jamie's pyjama sleeve. "We're stuck here, waiting for the Gnome to get us. We're trapped!"

"We'll find a way, Harry," Jamie said, forcing down his fear.

They crawled on, Jamie in front, spluttering in the dust, cobwebs trailing against his face. The tunnel started to dip downward and became smaller and narrower. *We must be inside the walls of the house now*, thought Jamie. He found he had to fight for breath – his chest felt tight, as if it were being squashed by the brick walls that seemed to be closing in on him. He could hear scuttling sounds, too. *I just hope that's mice.*

"Urgh! There're even more cobwebs now," said Milly. "Thicker ones. Stickier, too."

Jamie pulled some of the sticky threads away from his hands and face.

"The Gnome's spider's coming for us!" Harry's voice sounded small and frightened. "We'll be trapped in a giant web!" He pushed past Jamie and Milly and set off at a faster pace.

The rasping, scraping sound began again, growing louder.

"The tunnel's going to move again," shouted Jamie. "Quick!"

"No – wait," said Milly. In the darkness, Jamie could just see her outstretched finger pointing to some of the bricks in the tunnel wall. They were moving backwards, leaving dark holes. Jamie heard a sucking, squelching sound and jets of slimy goo shot out of them.

"What—" he began, just as Milly screamed.

She was clawing at her hair: something was stuck to her plaits, glowing faintly green.

"It's a spider's web!" Milly shouted. "Coming through the wall!"

"It's here!" Harry cried. "The spider must be here – it's trying to grab us with its web! It's going to get us!"

Jamie could see more thick strands bursting through the holes in the wall. The web stuck to him, glowing with a dim green light, and clung to his hands as he tried to brush it away. What size spider could spin a web this thick?

The sticky coils were all around them now, pulling at their hair and clothes. The web's greenish glow lit up their frightened faces. It shrank back, dragging Milly towards one of the holes in the wall. Jamie clawed a thick rope of it away from his arm, yanking Milly free.

"It's got me!" shouted Harry.

Jamie pulled a gluey strand from Harry's legs. "Come on, Harry."

"Keep moving," said Milly, tearing at the web and pushing at Jamie.

They struggled along the downward-sloping tunnel. In the green glow, Jamie could see Harry in front of him, swiping desperately at the web, panting with effort. "Keep going, Harry," Jamie called. "Just a little—"

But he stopped. Harry had disappeared. Jamie swiped his arms in front of him, panic rising in his chest. Nothing but empty space – and a large hole in the floor of the tunnel. "Harry!" Jamie cried.

Carefully, he and Milly crawled forward,

peering down into the hole. Harry's pale, soot-smudged face looked back. He was clinging to the rungs of a ladder.

"The ladder leads down the hole," said Jamie. "We can use it to get out of here! Harry, let me go first."

Harry moved to let Jamie climb down. Milly peered down after them. "Is that light down there?" she asked.

"It must be a room! Maybe this tunnel has taken us back inside the house. All we have to do to escape is climb down," Jamie said, grinning with relief.

But his smile faded as he saw Milly's worried face. "Look," she said, pointing just to the side of the ladder. They all turned. The cruel, sneering face of the Gnome was carved into the bricks.

Jamie shivered. "Gnome picture or not, it's the only way out," he said, swinging himself onto the ladder. The sound of evil cackling echoed around them.

"*Beware the spider's embrace!*" said a shrill voice. It was the Gnome.

Jamie gulped. "Come on," he said.

First Jamie, then Harry, then Milly set off down the ladder. Down, down they climbed, feeling with their feet for a grip on the rung below. *Surely we must be near the bottom,* thought Jamie. But when he looked past his feet, the light still seemed far away. *It's as if we've climbed down through the walls of Gnome Garden, and now we're deep underneath the house. . .*

"Help!" cried Harry, his foot sliding off the rung.

Jamie reached up to steady him, grabbing his brother's foot and placing it back onto the ladder. His gaze caught a movement beyond Harry and Milly, at the top of the ladder. Something was crouched over it.

In the dim light, Jamie could see a massive, round body. He gulped as he made out legs covered in bristling hairs. The creature opened its jaws with a sucking sound and a glob of green, glowing liquid dripped down the chimney. Eight round eyes glinted in the dim light.

The spider had arrived.

CHAPTER SIX

The Gnome's Trap

"Quick!" shouted Jamie, clambering desperately down the ladder. He missed a rung and slid some of the way, looking up to check for Harry and Milly above him.

"Jamie!" Milly yelled. "It's coming after us!"

"Faster! It's going to get us!" Harry cried.

Two long, hairy legs felt for the sides of the tunnel; then the spider squeezed his body into the opening. The light glinted in its eight blank eyes. It was huge — it had to force itself down the tunnel, legs squashing against the sides as it inched towards them. Jamie could see the bristling hairs on its body, tipped with gold. Its vicious-looking jaws snapped open and shut, revealing knife-sharp teeth.

"Come on!" shouted Jamie to the other two. "Just a bit further down the ladder, we'll be safe."

"That's what you think," replied a cruel voice from beneath them. Jamie looked down between his feet and saw a red, shiny face gazing up at him, two yellow eyes narrowed in evil delight.

"The Gnome," whimpered Harry.

Jamie gulped. They were trapped.

"You escaped last time," the Gnome snarled. "You won't get away this time. Have you ever seen a spider devour its prey? They eat little flics like you. *Alive.*"

Jamie felt the blood drain from his face and realized he was trembling with fear. They were stuck on the ladder between the vicious spider and a gnome who had sworn revenge on them. He looked up at Harry and Milly and saw that they were shaking too.

"We can't go up and we can't go down," whimpered Harry.

Suddenly the spider lunged at them. Its slicing jaws just missed the top of Milly's head as she darted to one side. Jamie saw a trail of green drool drip from its mouth into the darkness below.

"Down!" he shouted. "Come on!" He clambered down the ladder as fast as he could, Harry and Milly following. The spider made that horrible squelching sound again as it gnashed its jaws, squeezing itself down the chimney after them. The spider's red eyes glowed in the darkness, drawing closer.

"Hurry!" Milly's voice was hoarse with fear.

Jamie slid down the rest of the ladder, missing the rungs completely. He tumbled off the end into a vast cavern. In the centre of the cavern was a deep pit with a gigantic spider's web stretched across it. Jamie landed in a heap right at the edge of the web, and he dug his fingers into the rock to claw himself away from it. The web glowed with an eerie green light. *It must have been spun by the Gnome's creature*, he realized.

"Jamie!" cried Harry. He and Milly fell off the end of the ladder too, landing beside Jamie. All three of them stared at the web, transfixed.

"Where are we?" whispered Harry, his body shaking.

"Underground, I think," said Jamie. "Underneath Gnome Gardens."

"Isn't this nice?" said a mocking voice. The Gnome was standing on the other side of the web, his filthy toenails almost touching it. Beside him was a gleaming pile of shiny objects. He was staring at them, rubbing his bony hands together, his eyes glowing, full of hate. Jamie saw a spider crawl out from underneath his cap.

"You're just in time for dinner. There wasn't enough meat on the jackdaw for a creature as big as my spider," the Gnome continued, with a yellow-toothed smile. "She's still peckish. How good of you to come!"

There was a hissing sound, and Jamie saw the spider's bristling front legs and pincers emerge from the tunnel.

"Wait, my beauty," called the Gnome. "You'll get your meal soon enough." The spider stopped where it was, but its legs twitched horribly, ready to scuttle after them at the Gnome's command.

He began caressing the objects in the bright pile next to him, turning them in the light to admire them. Jamie could see glinting knives, a silver picture frame, one of Dad's spanners. And there was Mum's cheese grater.

"Look!" said Harry. "He's got my silver car!"

"What are you doing with our stuff?" demanded Jamie.

The Gnome snapped his gaze towards them, putting down a shiny teaspoon. All the things he'd collected sparkled. *He's stealing as many of our things as he can*, Jamie thought. He remembered how angry the Gnome had been that they were living in his house. *Is he stealing our stuff as revenge?*

"I could ask you the same question," the Gnome snarled. "You have something that belongs to me. And I want it back. *Now!*"

He spat the last word, and held his wrinkled hand out towards them.

"He must mean the scissors," whispered Milly, feeling inside her pocket. "Let's just give them to him and get out of here."

But Jamie saw a rope of green drool fall from the spider's pincers. He shook his head. "The Gnome's not going to let us go, even if we do hand them over," he whispered. "We're not giving you anything, Gnome!" he shouted, with more courage than he felt.

The Gnome gave an ugly laugh that echoed through the cavern. His eyes glittered cruelly. "Then what are we waiting for?" He turned to the spider. "Dinner time!"

The creature's eight bristly legs pulled its huge body out of the chimney, its vicious jaws working with a sucking sound. It hung above them, pincers dripping with green slime, its hairy legs hunched next to an enormous, gleaming body. Another glob of green saliva splashed right by Jamie's foot.

The spider spun a thick coil of green web from its underbelly, pulling it out of its body with its back legs and fixing it to the ladder. Then it swung down towards them.

They scrambled back, but Jamie soon felt the edge of the hole where the web was beneath his bare feet.

The Gnome laughed again. "Which one of you will my creature eat first, I wonder?"

Harry was shaking with fear. "I don't want to be eaten," he whimpered.

"We have to jump," Jamie said.

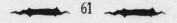

"Into the web?" Milly's voice trembled.

Jamie turned to look at the giant web. "We've no choice," he said. He grabbed Milly's hand on one side and Harry's on the other. "One, two, three. . ."

CHAPTER SEVEN

Inside the Spider's Lair

Jamie felt his stomach lurch as they leapt down towards the glowing web. The three of them landed with a bounce, then stuck fast. Ripples of movement spread across the web, out to the cavern walls.

The web felt gluey against Jamie's skin as he struggled to free himself. Milly's long plaits were ensnared, so that she could hardly lift her head. Harry kicked his legs to free them of the sticky strands, writhing about desperately, but he only became more entangled.

"There's no point struggling," sneered the Gnome. "You're not going to escape." He looked even more ghoulish lit from below by the green glow of the web. Jamie could see spiders scuttling out of his shirt pockets and down his collar. The Gnome sat down and bared his sharp yellow teeth at them.

The spider dropped down onto the web, making it shake violently. Its hairy legs were as thick as his own chest, while slime oozed from the red, yellow and green diamond on its round back. Worst of all was the way its eight eyes glittered as they fixed on its prey, above its gnashing, razor-sharp jaws. . .Jamie had to get them out of here!

"Milly – the scissors!" he shouted, as an idea came to him. "Can you reach them?"

"Of course!" said Milly, struggling to reach into her pyjama pocket. She brought out the shining silver scissors, the red jewel gleaming in the dim light.

The Gnome bellowed with rage. "My treasure! Give those back, you thief!" He turned to the spider. "Get them," he spat, saliva flying from his mouth. "Bind them up in your web and suck the life out of them."

The spider hissed and started to move towards them. But Milly snipped the scissors through the web, slicing a long tear that made the web lurch and ripple. Jamie and

Harry pulled at it, unravelling a gash right across the centre of the web. It was too weak to take the spider's weight, and the creature scuttled to the edge of the web.

"It's working!" cried Harry, his eyes wide in his pale face.

The Gnome's face was twisted with rage, his gnarled hands clenched into fists. "Attack!" he yelled.

The spider moved towards them, round the edge of the web. Its eight red eyes seemed fixed on Jamie, glinting wickedly.

"Quick!" he said, grabbing a section of the web in front of the spider's path. "Milly, cut here!"

Milly pulled her arm free of the sticky strands and snipped with the scissors again. The web swung wildly, quivering over the darkness below, but the spider didn't stop. It advanced on Milly, jaws open, preparing to sink its sharp, venomous teeth into her flesh. Jamie could see it reaching out with its front legs to grab its prey.

"Get away from her!" shouted Harry, struggling to free his arms and legs.

"Come on, Milly," urged Jamie. "Only another few cuts and you'll break the web!"

Milly cut through another sticky strand and suddenly the web split in two — Milly, Jamie and Harry on one side, the spider on the other. Each half of the web collapsed against the side of the cavern, slamming Jamie and the others into the wall. His stomach lurched as he looked down into the blackness below them. They were held fast by the sticky strands – but for how long?

Across the cavern, the spider climbed up the other half of the broken web. It was hissing angrily; one of its eight legs was bent at an awkward angle. It heaved its massive body onto the ledge, then shot a sticky strand of web to a wooden beam in the roof of the cavern. It swung there, watching them.

"Hurt my creature, have you?" said the Gnome, his face contorted with fury. "That doesn't mean you're going to escape."

The Gnome rummaged through the pile of shiny objects until he found Dad's spanner. Then he went to the section of web Jamie, Harry and Milly were suspended from. His gaze fixed greedily on the scissors in Milly's hand; the red stones embedded in their handles were shining. "My treasure," he spat.

He hooked the spanner through the web and began to draw it up, hand over hand.

"He's dragging us up," said Harry, his lips quivering. "We can't escape this time!"

"*Heave!*" The Gnome chanted to himself, the muscles working in his arms. With judders and jerks, they were being pulled up through the air.

Jamie looked around desperately, when his elbow suddenly struck something hard. Rungs! A thin, spindly ladder extended from somewhere beneath them, up out of the hole, along the cavern walls and out of a gap in the corner of the ceiling. It was so slender, hidden away against the wall, that Jamie hadn't seen it until now. It looked fragile. Would it be strong enough to hold them? *We'll just have to try*, he thought.

"Harry! Milly!" he whispered, clinging to the web as the Gnome gave another *heave*. "Look – that's our way out."

Milly frowned, her plaits tangled in the web. "But how?"

"My survival kit!" said Harry, turning awkwardly so Jamie could get at it.

"It's our only chance," said Jamie. He glanced up – they were inching towards the Gnome, whose eyes sparked dangerously in the dim light. Jamie had to be careful not to let him see. One-handed, he slid the zip open, then felt around inside. He tried to imagine what would distract the Gnome. He liked shiny things. . .

"*Heave!*" said the Gnome.

"Hurry, Jamie," Milly said.

He took out the sandy bucket. Harry's bag of crisps fell out of the backpack and plummeted down into the darkness below them. Jamie pushed his hand right to the bottom of the backpack. He could feel the coarse fabric of Dad's gardening gloves, and underneath them the net bag of chocolate coins, in their gold wrappers. *Can we use these to trick the Gnome?* Jamie wondered. Carefully, he emptied the coins into the bucket, using Harry's body as a shield so that the Gnome couldn't see.

With a final grunt, their enemy hauled the web onto the stone surface of the cavern. Jamie, Harry and Milly lay in front of the Gnome. They'd never been this close to him before. Jamie could see each of the wispy hairs on his chin, the spiders scuttling among the folds of his filthy clothes. His breath smelled dank and rotten, like a dirty, stagnant pond.

The Gnome looked at them coldly. "Now. Where's my treasure?"

CHAPTER EIGHT

Escape from the Cavern

"Here's your treasure," Jamie said. He held up the plastic bucket full of gold-covered chocolate coins, offering it to the Gnome. "A crock of pure gold!"

The Gnome's sneer became a horrible smile. He licked his lips as he reached out a claw-like hand and snatched the bucket greedily, carrying it a few paces away. He dipped into it and ran his hands through the coins. "Gold!" he muttered. His lips curled in an ugly grin.

As the Gnome lovingly held up one of the largest coins, stroking its shiny wrapper, Jamie whispered to Harry and Milly. "Come on – let's cut ourselves free while the Gnome's distracted."

Milly snipped through the spider's web, cutting it from their hair and clothes, until it fell to the ground.

"To the ladder!" Jamie whispered.

But the Gnome gave a roar. "I haven't finished with you yet!" He bounded towards them.

"The web!" yelled Jamie. "Quick, Harry – I need Dad's gardening gloves!"

Harry opened his backpack and tossed him the gloves. Jamie pulled them on and picked up the sticky web. He threw it at the Gnome, the gloves flying from his hands as they stuck fast to the gooey surface. The web closed on the Gnome like a net, trapping him. As he struggled, he became more entangled in its threads. "Curse you!" he screamed, thrashing about. "Thieves!"

"Quick!" called Jamie, running to the ladder, pulling the others after him.

From the corner of his eye he saw the giant spider moving its legs, one of them dangling limply, as it hung on its thread.

"Get them!" shouted the Gnome.

They scrambled up the ladder as fast as they could, first Jamie, then Harry, then Milly. The thin rungs bowed under their weight, but held as they heaved themselves up. The Gnome's muffled curses followed them as they went.

"We've done it!" Jamie shouted, grinning with relief.

But Harry gave a yell of fear. "Help!" he cried.

Jamie looked down to see a thick, sticky thread caught on his brother's backpack. The spider hung menacingly beneath them in the cavern. It cast another thread, which stuck to Harry's pyjama top.

"Do something!" cried Harry, as the spider began to reel the web in, tugging Harry's legs off the ladder.

Jamie leaned down and grabbed Harry's hand. "Milly!" he called. "Cut Harry free!"

She was already moving towards Harry.

She squeezed herself onto the ladder next to him.

"Ha!" shouted the Gnome. He had torn the last of the web from his scrawny body. "My creature will get you, you fools!"

Harry had locked his arms behind the rungs. His legs kicked the air, struggling to get back to the ladder. Jamie clenched his fingers around his brother's wrist.

Milly held on to the ladder with one hand and reached out as far as she could with the other, scissors at the ready. She snipped.

First one thread snapped, then the other. Harry slammed back against the ladder.

"Let's go!" Milly shouted.

"Attack!" bellowed the Gnome. His voice sounded so loud in the echoing cavern that

Jamie's ears hurt. "Suck their blood! Eat them alive!"

A sticky thread whizzed past Jamie's head, just missing him. He looked down. The spider was crawling slowly up the wall beneath them, dragging its injured leg.

"It's after us!" cried Milly.

Jamie climbed faster, and saw that they were nearly at the narrow gap in the cavern ceiling. "There's a tunnel ahead," he called to the others.

"It's gaining on me!" Milly shouted, scrambling up the ladder behind Jamie and Harry. "Hurry!"

Jamie could hear the revolting sucking of the spider's dripping jaws as he hauled himself through the gap. It was only just wide enough for him to turn around to pull Harry through. *Too narrow for the spider*, he thought with relief. Both boys reached out an arm to help Milly, who was still scrambling up the last rungs of the ladder.

"Milly, look out!" yelled Jamie, as the spider's jaws snapped shut on one of her long plaits.

She wheeled round to face the creature, the scissors poised, and lunged at its eyes. "Take *that*!"

There was a horrible squelch. The spider lurched backwards, giving Milly just enough time to wriggle into the tunnel with Jamie and Harry. The spider began to hiss and gurgle in pain.

From somewhere below them, they heard the Gnome's cries of fury. "I'll have my revenge!" he yelled. "I'll defeat you!"

Jamie pulled Harry along behind him. "Let's get out of this place," he said.

They crawled along the tunnel single file, Milly leading the way. "It's sloping upward," she yelled. "It's taking us back into Gnome Gardens!"

The tunnel climbed higher and higher. Then it stopped, and dropped sharply downward. It was sooty and there was a ladder on its wall.

"We're back inside one of the chimney flues," Jamie realized. Rather than the ghoulish green glow of the spider's web, a warm, welcoming light glimmered at the bottom. "It's a room," he said. "We're safe!"

One of the bottom rungs was missing, and Milly slipped down with a cry, followed by Jamie and Harry. They tumbled into an empty grate and rolled onto the floorboards in a cloud of soot.

Jamie, Harry and Milly sat blinking at one another. Their faces and pyjamas were covered in grime. Harry's arm was cut and his faced grazed. A dark bruise had begun to bloom on Milly's temple. She was holding her plaits in front of her, one of them cut off at shoulder length, tipped with green slime.

"How am I going to explain this to my mum and dad?" she asked.

Jamie shook his head, sending soot drifting onto the carpet. "We'd better say we were trying to rescue a bird that flew up the chimney."

Milly laughed. "That's sort of true."

Above them a sliver of moon shone through the coloured glass in the ceiling.

"We're in Granddad's study!" Jamie said. The room was lined with dusty books, and in the middle stood Granddad's huge wooden desk. Jamie noticed the oval panel that stood out from the rest of the wooden carvings in the room. Inside it were five carved creatures — a snake and a spider were the first two. Jamie remembered that the first time he'd seen it, all the creatures had been in profile. Then the snake had turned to face inwards into the room.

"First a giant snake, now a giant spider. We have to stop the Gnome," Jamie said.

"How, though?" Harry's filthy face looked ghostly in a patch of yellow light.

"He likes treasure, shiny things," Milly said. "That could help us."

"He's trying to steal all the precious things in the house," Jamie said. "Maybe—"

He was cut short by a grinding sound. It was coming from the oval panel. They all turned to look: the spider carving shifted, turning to face inwards into the room. It stopped. Eight jewelled eyes glimmered in the dim light.

"Just like the snake carving," Jamie said. "It's as if they're watching us, planning something. . ."

"I guess that's the Gnome's next creature." Harry was pointing at the animal next to the spider.

It was carved in mid-flight, its mouth open to reveal a row of tiny sharp teeth.

Jamie felt a fluttering in his stomach, like the flapping of leathery wings. "A bat," he said. "After what we did to his spider, I bet the Gnome makes sure it's a mean one."

"He's going to want even more revenge," said Harry. "At first, he just wanted us out of his house. Now, he'll want to get even with us."

"We'd better be ready for him next time," agreed Milly.

"We have to be brave," Jamie said. "If we stick together, we'll defeat him. No matter what he does to us."

Jamie hoped he was right. After all, another creature would be waiting for them. . .

Join Jamie, Harry and Milly in the
next CREEPY CREATURES adventure!

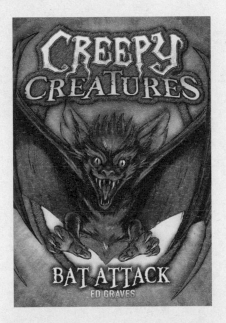

Turn the page for a sneak preview. . .

CHAPTER ONE

A Storm at Gnome Gardens

A fork of lightning raced across the afternoon sky, lighting up the turrets and gargoyles of Gnome Gardens. Jamie looked up at the enormous old house, with its ivy-covered walls and windows like scowling eyes. He found it hard to believe that it was his home now. Then – *crash!* – a great roll of thunder boomed in his ears. Rain burst from the swollen clouds, drenching him, his brother Harry, and their friend, Milly.

"Quick!" Milly shouted, her hair plastered to her face by the rain. "Get inside!" She ran for the path.

Jamie threw down his rake. The three of them had been tidying the neglected vegetable patch in Jamie and Harry's vast, overgrown garden. Now rain water turned the earth to thick mud, washing away the seeds they'd planted. A sudden gust of wind sent the cracked windows of the greenhouse rattling in their frames.

Jamie squelched through the soil to join Milly. His muddy trainers slipped on the wet moss on the paving stones.

"Come on, Harry!" he called to his brother.

Harry was still standing in the sticky mud, staring up at the sky and hugging his arms to his chest. Jamie shivered as the wind howled around him, bending the trees and tearing the leaves from their branches. The leaves swooped and fluttered through the air, like a flock of tiny creatures in the gloomy sky.

"Bats!" Harry shouted, as the leaves swirled. "They've come to get us already!" He ran towards Jamie and Milly, mud splattering his jeans.

"Harry, they're just leaves!" Jamie called, shouting to be heard above the wind.

But Jamie knew why his brother was scared of seeing bats. In the study at the centre of Gnome Gardens, the boys had found *The Book of Gnome*, which was written by Jamie and Harry's grandad. They'd read in the book about the evil Gnome who thought he owned their house. The Gnome had already sent two of his creepy creatures to drive them out – a monstrous snake and a spider. The book's ancient pages had shown them that the next creature they would meet was an evil-looking, yellow-eyed bat, its leathery wings outstretched, its ugly snout curled into a snarl that revealed sharp fangs. Underneath the picture was a single line: *Fear the bats up above.* Jamie shivered. No wonder Harry was so jumpy.

"Hurry up," Jamie said. He led his brother and Milly as they slithered up the path.

All three of them cried out as a fork of

lightning shot down in front of them. The old, dead tree in the middle of the garden sizzled. They froze, staring at the smoking branches, a great roar of thunder echoing in their ears.

There was a loud crack.

"Look out!" shouted Jamie, grabbing Milly and Harry and pulling them backwards. A huge branch fell from the tree and crashed to the ground, missing them by inches.

Milly's face was white with shock. "Thanks. That was a close one." She grabbed Harry's hand and with the other pushed Jamie along. "Let's go. We have to get inside before the lightning strikes again."

"This is just the sort of time the Gnome would choose to come for us," Harry said, the rain running down his face and dripping off the end of his nose. "The middle of a storm."

Jamie saw his brother reach behind him for the backpack he always carried. It contained his "survival kit" – odds and ends that Harry thought might be useful. Jamie was sure that, no matter what Harry had put in it this time, none of it would be much use if the Gnome attacked now. The three of them had vowed to defeat him, but Jamie didn't want to have to try in the middle of a raging storm.

They reached the end of the path. Gnome Gardens was on top of the hill, but Milly's cottage was through a gate on the other side of the garden.

"I'll see you tomorrow," Milly shouted over the storm. "Don't stand under any trees –

you've more chance of being struck by lightning. And keep low to the ground!"

"Be careful, Milly!" shouted Harry.

But before she left the path, a chilling sound rose above the howling wind and lashing rain. The three of them stared, open-mouthed, at one another.

It was the unmistakable sound of the Gnome's evil laughter.

LOOK OUT

for the other books

in the series. . .

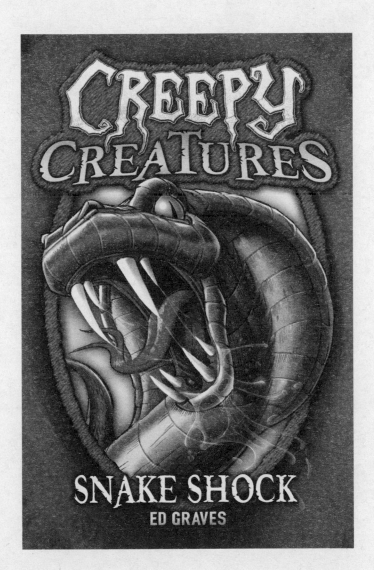

CREEPY CREATURES

SNAKE SHOCK

ED GRAVES

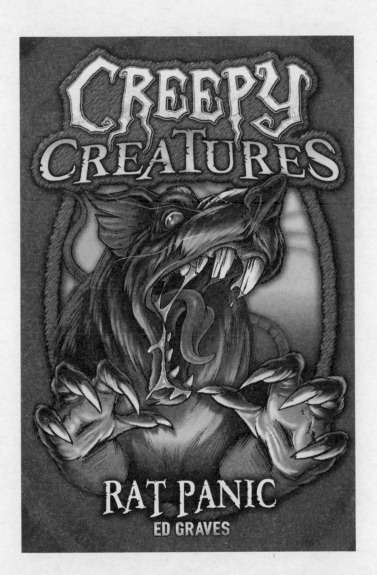